Sure as Strawberries

Story by Sue Ann Alderson
Illustrations by Karen Reczuch

NORTHERN
LIGHTS BOOKS FOR CHILDREN

Red Deer College Press

Every summer Mattie visited her Uncle George, and that was her favorite time in the whole year.

Uncle George kept twenty-eight goats. He named them all and brushed their coats and took them for rides in his car. They were the friendliest goats in the world. Mattie loved them.

Uncle George was a water diviner; he had the gift. "The gift runs deep and hidden," Uncle George would say. "It's there to be found like water, like a good friend, sure as strawberries."

When a neighbor needed a new well, Uncle George would take a forked willow wand and walk slowly over the land, holding the wand straight out before him, each hand grasping one side of the fork. As he walked, he'd coax the wand with his special charm:

> *"Willow wand, willow wand,*
> *betwixt, between, beneath, beyond,*
> *find the winding water, find*
> *the deep and hidden stream."*

Then, sure as strawberries, the tip of the wand would dip and bobble and tug and finally curve in a graceful arc toward the earth. When folks took their shovels and dug deep down at the exact spot where the wand had pointed, they found water. Many's the well Uncle George had found, and he never took money for it.

"That would break the power, spoil the charm," Uncle George would say.

So folks gave him feed and straw for his goats, vegetables from their gardens, or sometimes a quilt or some clothes they had made. And if they didn't have anything like that, they would go to the mountain meadows and pick a pail of the wild berries that grew plentiful and free, and they would make jam or bake muffins for Uncle George. But best of all, they gave Uncle George their friendship.

"Friendship is precious as water," Uncle George would say.

Mattie loved watching Uncle George find water. Sometimes when he was busy, Mattie would go off by herself and cut a forked willow branch and practice. She held the wand firmly straight out in front of her and coaxed it with the charm:

> *"Willow wand, willow wand,*
> *betwixt, between, beneath, beyond,*
> *find the winding water, find*
> *the deep and hidden stream."*

Sometimes the tip would dip and bobble a bit, but it never did arc to the ground. And dig as she might, Mattie never did find water.

"Maybe I just don't have the gift," Mattie once said to Uncle George.
"Maybe you don't, but maybe you do," he told her. "The gift sometimes
starts out tiny as a berry seed. It needs some nourishing before it grows."

Then came the hard, hot summer when the wells dried up and Uncle George took a fall. He broke his arm and had to wear a cast from his shoulder to his fingertips.

Neighbors hauled water from town for him, but twenty-eight goats needed more water than the neighbors could haul.

"If I could look for water, I could find a new well," Uncle George told Mattie. He took his favorite willow wand to look for water near the orchard, but before long he was home again, looking discouraged. "I can't feel the wand with this bad arm. And I can't let the goats go thirsty."

Friends offered to keep one or two goats for him over the dry spell, but no one could keep all twenty-eight. "I'll have to sell them," said Uncle George. "There's no way out."

It was a sad time for him.

It was a sad time for Mattie too. There were only three days before she was to leave for home. The goats were Uncle George's family, and hers too. If only I could find water, she thought, that would do the trick.

She'd never found water before, but there was always a chance, and it was the only chance they had. She didn't tell Uncle George her plan because she didn't want him to be disappointed if she failed.

The next morning, Mattie rose really early. She found the best wand ever and went divining up the hill behind the barn:

> *"Willow wand, willow wand,*
> *betwixt, between, beneath, beyond,*
> *find the winding water, find*
> *the deep and hidden stream."*

The wand dipped and bobbled and suddenly curved in a graceful arc toward the earth.

Very excited, Mattie started to dig. She dug for a very long time; then her shovel struck something hard. She brushed away the dirt with her hands and uncovered a rusty old metal drum. Just a hunk of old metal, thought Mattie, no good at all! She thumped it with her shovel and slosh! What did Mattie hear? Quickly she whacked a hole in the metal. The container was half full of water.

"It's not exactly a well," said Mattie, "but it *is* water. I just need to find more."

Then it was time for Uncle George to be getting up, so Mattie hid her wand and shovel and went back to the house.

The next morning, Mattie rose really early again and took her best wand ever to the furthest corner of the pasture to the west. Here Mattie had to push through thick brush and thorny brambles, but she didn't turn back. Where things grow, there's water underground, she thought, and pushed on.

> *"Willow wand, willow wand,*
> *betwixt, between, beneath, beyond,*
> *find the winding water, find*
> *the deep and hidden stream,"*

she coaxed over and over. Finally—the wand dipped and bobbled again and arced to the ground.

Mattie dug and dug, even longer than before, and finally she unearthed stones set in a circle. She had seen such things on other farms with Uncle George, so she knew she'd found the original well for the farm, long ago abandoned, filled in and overgrown.

There wasn't enough water in it then and there wouldn't be now, thought Mattie. But at least the wand did find more water. At least I know it's possible.

Mattie only had the rest of that day to find water. If she didn't, Uncle George would lose the goats forever.

So, when he walked out to the mail box at mid-morning, she tried, and when he had an afternoon nap, she tried again, but she had no luck. Finally, there was just the evening left.

"After we're done with supper," said Mattie, passing the mashed potatoes, "I'd like to walk the logging road one more time—a blue flower grows there I'd like to take home for pressing."

"I'd go with you, but that's too far for me with this arm. Take a goat for company," said Uncle George.

"All right," said Mattie.

It was a long walk over the old road to the east meadow. All along the
way, Mattie held the wand straight out and coaxed:

> "Willow wand, willow wand,
> betwixt, between, beneath, beyond,
> find the winding water, find
> the deep and hidden stream."

It was a far, far way to go; the wand did not dip and bob at all. Mattie was
almost ready to give up.

Then, at the edge of the east meadow, Mattie felt the wand strain slightly to one side, so she turned that way and said the charm again as she walked very, very slowly, one step at a time:

> *"Willow wand, willow wand,*
> *betwixt, between, beneath, beyond,*
> *find the winding water, find*
> *the deep and hidden stream."*

Suddenly, sure as strawberries, the wand dipped and bobbled and curved, twitched, tugged, pulled and swerved in a true arc pointing to the earth. Mattie was so surprised by the power of the pull, she almost tumbled.

Down she dug—and dug, and dug. At first the earth was slightly damp, then damper, thoroughly moist. Mattie's arms were so tired they felt ready to fall off, but she kept digging till she scooped up mud—lovely, oozing wet and watery mud!

Mattie ran all the way back.

"Uncle George!" she called, seeing him in the yard. Gasping for breath, she told him, and he went with her, as quickly as he could, to see the wet place.

"It looks like a spring," said Uncle George. "I'll call the neighbors to give us a hand digging, and if it doesn't peter out, you've found a good well and saved us all!" He put his good arm around her and squeezed her shoulder.

When the neighbors came and dug, the water did not peter out. It was an underground spring Mattie had found, fine for a well with plenty of water for twenty-eight goats.

"You have the gift, Mattie," said Uncle George. He was happy, and Mattie was happy, and so were all the neighbors. The goats were happy too.

"Next summer," Uncle George said that afternoon when he put Mattie on the train for home, "next summer we'll go out together, you and I, when people want water found. We'll be the best team of diviners folks have ever seen!"

And sure as strawberries, they were.

For my ever-loving parents, Ruth E. and Eugene L. Hartley,
who gave me the goatman, the dowser, and so much else,
and for my ever-loving children, Rebecca and Kai, who are
the best gifts, sure as strawberries!
–SUE ANN ALDERSON

For my Corrin.
–KAREN RECZUCH

NORTHERN LIGHTS BOOKS FOR CHILDREN ARE PUBLISHED BY
Red Deer College Press
56 Avenue & 32 Street Box 5005
Red Deer Alberta Canada T4N 5H5

ACKNOWLEDGEMENTS
Edited for the Press by Tim Wynne-Jones
Printed and bound in Canada by D.W. Friesen Ltd.
for Red Deer College Press
The Publishers gratefully acknowledge the financial
assistance of the Alberta Foundation for the Arts,
Alberta Culture & Multiculturalism, The Canada Council,
Red Deer College, and Radio 7 CKRD

CANADIAN CATALOGUING IN PUBLICATION DATA
Alderson, Sue Ann, 1940–
(Northern Lights Books for Children)
ISBN 0-88995-087-3
I. Reczuch, Karen, 1956– II. Title. III. Series.
PS8551.L44S9 1992 jC813'.54 C92-091323-7
PZ7.A43Su 1992

PLYMOUTH PUBLIC SCHOOL
111 First Street
Welland, Ontario L3B 4S1
(905) 732-4110